A DAY THAT CHANGED AMERICA

# EARTHQUAKE!

APRIL 18, 1906

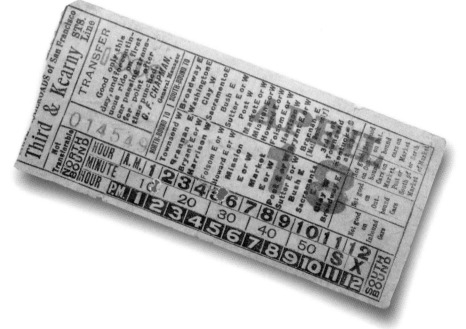

Text, Design, and Compilation
© 2004 The Madison Press Limited
Paintings © 2004 David Craig

First published in the United States by

Hyperion Books for Children
114 Fifth Avenue
New York, New York
10011-5690

First U.S. edition, 2004

1 3 5 7 9 10 8 6 4 2

Library of Congress Cataloging-in-Publication Data is on file.

ISBN 0-7868-1882-4

(Previous page) A streetcar transfer that was issued at 5:10 A.M. on
April 18, 1906 — just three minutes before the Great Earthquake.

Printed in Singapore

# A DAY THAT CHANGED AMERICA

# EARTHQUAKE!

*On a Peaceful Spring Morning, Disaster Strikes San Francisco*

TEXT BY SHELLEY TANAKA ✢ PAINTINGS BY DAVID CRAIG

*Historical consultation by Gladys Hansen*

Hyperion Books for Children

A HYPERION / MADISON PRESS BOOK

# Wednesday, April 18, 1906

It was still dark. Dawn had not yet broken, and most of San Francisco was fast asleep.

Yet something was wrong. In the stockyards by the railway tracks, a pack of longhorn steer bellowed, pressing against the sides of their pens. Outside a mansion on Nob Hill, a dog began to bark. In a stable south of Market Street, fire horses stomped and tossed their heads.

A flock of starlings burst out of the trees in Golden Gate Park. Across town, above the ferry docks, the gulls wheeled and screamed.

And then the ground itself began to heave.

The majestic Call Building, left, rises above the peaceful city of San Francisco in this panorama from 1905. (Inset) A period postcard shows Market Street, with the Call Building in the distance.

# CHAPTER ONE

# EARTHQUAKE!

HUGH KWONG LIANG WAS DREAMING. HE WAS ON A BOAT, BEING TOSSED ON A WILD SEA while waves crashed around him and giant drops of water slapped against his face. He opened his eyes. It was black as coal in his room behind the family grocery store in Chinatown. Cousin Lung Tin was shaking him and screaming, and the entire room was trembling. Pieces of plaster and wood were falling from the ceiling.

Hugh quickly pulled on his clothes and ran into the store. Boxes of dried fish and gingerroot had crashed from the counter. Crates of bamboo shoots had overturned onto the floor.

Hugh and Lung Tin ran outside just as the building across the street collapsed. Above them, power lines snapped and dropped to the ground, smoking and hissing like snakes.

They hurried down the street to Portsmouth Square, where panicky, noisy groups were already gathering. Some headed to the Kwong Chow Temple to burn incense and pray to Kwan Kung, the God of War, to protect them. Others cried that the Earth Dragon was unleashing his anger from below.

Seven blocks away, at the foot of Market Street, the clock on the tower of the Ferry Building had stopped at 5:13 A.M.

EVEN BEFORE SHE OPENED HER EYES, TEN-YEAR-OLD DORIS BEPLER THOUGHT THE END of the world had come. Just like in the stories she had read in Sunday school. When she peered out over her blankets, it was exactly as she had feared. Her familiar bedroom had gone mad. The gaslight hanging from the ceiling

❧

*(Left) The clock on the tower of the Ferry Building stopped at 5:13 A.M., the exact moment the earthquake struck. (Opposite) Hugh and his cousin scramble through upended baskets and barrels on their way out to the street.*

swung wildly back and forth. The picture of her mother was thrashing against the wall, twisting viciously on its wires.

Doris covered her face with her hands, scrunched up against her pillow, and rolled herself into a ball. Through her fingers she looked across at the bed where her older sister Louise was huddled. The window shades flew up into the room and slammed back down. The furniture danced. She saw the bedroom door slam shut, but she did not hear it over the roar of the trembling earth.

The quake lasted for less than a minute. Then everything went still.

Doris jumped out of bed and ran to the door. She grabbed the handle and pulled with all her might, but the frame had buckled, and the door was wedged shut. A hot, heavy feeling of panic rose up in her throat, and she thought she would scream.

Then she felt the doorknob rattle, the door miraculously opened, and there was her mother.

"That was a bad earthquake, wasn't it?" Mrs. Bepler said calmly. "Let's all get dressed as quickly as possible." Then her mother moved down the hall to the next room where Doris's younger sisters were struggling to pull open their door.

Doris's fingers trembled as she did up her buttons. Her toes wouldn't find the end of her stockings. When she tried to lace up her shoes, she pulled so hard that one of the laces broke.

She hobbled noisily down the hall to her parents' room.

"Mother," she called. "My shoe — "

"Hush," her mother said. "You'll wake the babies." She was shaking and folding diapers. Beside the big bed, Doris's baby sisters were sleeping peacefully.

The biggest earthquake in San Francisco's history hadn't even woken them up.

Downstairs, Mr. Bepler made cocoa on the coal-and-wood stove. Doris and her sisters were eating thick slices of bread and butter sprinkled with brown sugar when the doorbell rang. It was Cecil, the boy next door.

"A house fell down on Steiner Street," he shouted excitedly.

Doris didn't believe him. She followed him down the steps. As she closed the door behind her, she could hear her parents arguing in the kitchen. Mr. Bepler wanted to go downtown to check on his machine shop. But Doris's mother told him his duty was to be at home with his family. What would she do alone with six children if something happened to him?

❧

159. Wrecked Homes, Ninth and Brannan Sts, April 18, 1906, San Francisco, Cal.

Doris and Cecil cut through the park to Steiner Street. It was true. The big green house on the corner lay in a jumbled heap of splintered boards. The two women who lived there were sitting on the steps of the house next door wearing just their flannelette wrappers. Their hair was still in curlers. They were pulling on their stockings right there in the street!

They had woken up to feel their house leaning over, farther and farther. And they had only managed to stumble down the stairs and out onto the street before the whole building collapsed right behind them.

*(Above) A wooden house lies in ruins at 9th and Brannon Streets. (Below) Although some homes didn't crumble, they shifted so dangerously on their foundations that they were uninhabitable.*

SOL LESSER STOOD ON THE SIDEWALK OUTSIDE HIS HOUSE AT SUTTER AND LAGUNA. HE HAD lived in San Francisco all his life, and at sixteen he was used to earthquakes. The city usually had three or four light quakes a year. They lasted just long enough to wake you up or make the dishes rattle.

But this one was different. Heavier. It had tossed him right out of bed. And now that he was out in the street, he could see that people were really afraid. Some had come out of their houses barefoot and in their nightclothes. Men still had flecks of shaving cream on their faces.

His neighbors were trying to decide what to do. Was it safe to go back inside? Would there be aftershocks? Should they stand in a doorway? Stay out in the open in the park? Or just carry on as if nothing had happened?

Sol decided to carry on. He was due for his morning shift at the hardware store downtown, but the streetcars didn't seem to be running.

So he started to walk.

It was very quiet. People were standing in the street, their faces gray and staring.

As he walked he noticed more and more damage. Chimneys had fallen into the street. Past Van Ness Avenue the masonry was cracked on several houses, and some buildings had collapsed. People were digging frantically through the rubble, looking for their families, their neighbors.

At the corner of Bush Street, crowds were heading toward the California Hotel, just a block away. A brick chimney and the east wall of the hotel had fallen onto the fire hall next door, punching a hole right through the roof. Three floors of the fire station had come crashing down. People said the city's fire chief and his wife lay buried beneath the rubble.

When Sol reached Market Street, the situation was even worse. On the other side of the street, lodging houses and hotels had simply crumbled on top of their inhabitants like houses of cards.

Behind them, clouds of gray smoke were billowing up into the sky.

࿔

*(Above) A cable car on Sutter Street the year before the quake. (Opposite, top) Large cracks split the cobblestone streets, making it difficult for wagons and cars to move around the city. (Opposite, inset) Shocked homeowners and neighbors gather in front of a row of collapsed town houses.*

# CHAPTER TWO

# FIRE!

IGHT-YEAR-OLD DEWITT BALDWIN COULD HARDLY SIT STILL. HERE WAS HIS FAMILY calmly eating breakfast in their apartment on the edge of the Mission District. They were acting as if it were a morning like any other. As if they hadn't all been practically tossed from their beds by the earthquake. The house had rocked from side to side so violently that their heavy upright piano slid a foot and a half away from the wall. In the parlor, broken dishes and glasses were scattered on the floor.

Now DeWitt just wanted to go outside to see the damage.

After breakfast his father headed to his office. Mrs. Baldwin joined the neighbors on the street, exchanging reports about what was happening in the rest of the city. Someone said fires were blazing all over downtown.

DeWitt peered out the front window. His mother was on the sidewalk, holding his squirming baby sister and talking to the neighbors. She was too busy to notice when

*(Opposite) Flames lick at the homes on a hillside street as panicked residents flee the neighborhood. (Right) Smoke from the spreading fire rises over the Mission District.*

he slipped down the back stairs of the building and out onto the street.

It was hard for DeWitt to make his way downtown. Some roads were ripped apart by gaping holes. When DeWitt peered into them, he could sometimes see things — bricks, twisted metal, a shoe, a scurrying rat. Other times the crack was too deep and black to see anything at all. It looked as if it might lead straight down to the center of the planet.

When he came to Valencia Street, he stopped suddenly and stared down the block at the Valencia Street Hotel.

It looked as if the earth had tried to swallow the building whole. The bottom three floors had sunk into the ground, and the stores that used to line the sidewalk on the main floor had simply disappeared. The top story had fallen out into the street.

DeWitt looked down. His shoes were full of water. Right in front of the hotel, a water main had broken. Water was gushing onto the street and pouring into the buried hotel.

A huge crowd had gathered. One person claimed that more than a hundred people were trapped inside the hotel, probably drowned, or crushed to death. Another said he had seen a man climb out a fourth-floor window, stepping right onto the pavement. Nearby stood an old man surrounded by cages of canaries. He and his precious birds had been rescued from the top floor.

Neighbors broke into nearby stores to seize axes and ropes to help with the rescue effort. Workers ripped apart sections of the roof so they could pull out people who were trapped inside. Behind the hotel, policemen were clambering over tangled piles of boards and mattresses, looking for bodies.

DeWitt backed away and headed for a plume of smoke rising a few blocks away. At the corner of Mission Street and 22nd a crowd had gathered as firemen frantically battled the flames streaming out of a large department store.

VALENCIA ST. HOTEL. AP/6
COPYRIGHT. WHIGHAM. F

*(Above) Only the top floor of the Valencia Street Hotel is still recognizable. As many as two hundred people may have been trapped inside after the earthquake. (Inset) The Valencia photographed in 1898.*

*(Right) Throughout the city, firefighters battled blazes with dwindling supplies of water. They also risked their lives to rescue people trapped under the debris. (Inset) A firefighter and a volunteer struggle to free an injured man from the ruins of a collapsed building.*

All over the city, firefighters were facing their worst nightmares. A number of stations had been damaged by the earthquake. At one, the front doors were jammed shut, making it impossible to wheel out the equipment. At another, the doors had been jolted open and the fire horses had escaped.

In places the heat from the flames was so fierce that workers could not get near the hydrants. It was hard to find water. The earthquake had cracked the city's water mains. The underground cisterns were unmarked, and those that were found were quickly emptied. Even sewer water was used. Navy workers linked hoses to try to bring water a mile uphill from the bay, but it was slow, backbreaking work.

So the flames continued to rage and spread. And as the day wore on, it quickly became clear that fire, not the earthquake, would be the real enemy.

TO HUGH LIANG, IT SEEMED THAT EVERY PERSON IN CHINATOWN WAS CRAMMED INTO TINY Portsmouth Square. They were pouring out of the rickety wooden buildings — more people, it seemed, than Chinatown could possibly hold. Most were single men. They lived in dark, dingy boardinghouses, where narrow wooden bunks were nailed to the wall like shelves, and the men had to sleep in shifts because there weren't enough beds. In other buildings, families of six would occupy a tiny single room. There were no kitchens or bathrooms. People cooked in windowless halls, where smoke and soot stained the walls.

Hugh had grown up here, surrounded by the smells from the cigar factories and the fish markets, and the scent of ginger and onions from the vegetable stands. It was his home. During the day men would gather in his father's store, exchanging news from the Old Country, talking politics, and telling ghost stories. In the evenings the Chinese theater and five-cent movie house nearby were packed, and smoky basement rooms were filled with noisy mah-jongg games.

Yet many Chinese were bitterly disappointed by their lives here. Hugh's mother was one of them. Six years before, when Hugh was only nine, she took his younger sister and four brothers back to China. She said the Chinese would never be welcomed in America. Hugh stayed behind to help his father run the family grocery store. Then, just eight months ago, his father died, leaving an older cousin, Lung Tin, in charge of the store, with instructions that he should take care of Hugh and provide for the family back in China.

Hugh scanned the crowd for Cousin Lung Tin now.

Suddenly, a single longhorn steer came wheeling around the corner and plunged into the crowd. The sight filled the people of Chinatown with horror. Hugh had often listened to the Chinatown elders in his father's store recounting the ancient myths. One story claimed that the Earth was held up on the backs of four giant bulls.

Now those beasts had broken loose, and the very ground was crumbling.

The huge animal roared into the square, its eyes wild as the crowd scattered. There was a gash on its side and blood was streaming down its flank. A police officer appeared, raised his gun, and shot it.

People screamed that the world was coming to an end. They ran back into their houses. They threw bundles and boxes from windows and rooftops. Store owners hurried into their shops and gathered their money and goods. Vegetable peddlers rented out their horse-drawn wagons for outrageous prices.

Hugh spotted Lung Tin banging at the door of a truck. When Hugh ran over to him,

# Chinatown

By 1906, Chinese immigrants had been coming to California for more than fifty years. They came to escape desperately poor lives in China, to search for gold, and to work on the railroad.

San Francisco, the biggest port on the Pacific coast, was the first stop, and many Chinese stayed there, despite the discrimination they faced. After the railroad was completed, laws were passed to keep more Chinese from entering the country, and to prevent the ones already there from bringing their wives or marrying whites. Outside Chinatown, Chinese could not rent rooms, and they were often refused service in restaurants and barbershops. Some gave up their hope of a good life in the New World and returned to their native country. But for many, staying in America was still better than the life they faced in China.

Chinatown was a mostly poor, overcrowded district in the heart of San Francisco. Some immigrants thrived here as business owners, doctors, herbalists, landlords, and restaurant owners. But many others worked as peddlers, laundrymen, or houseboys or cooks for rich families, hoping to have enough money one day to return to China or start a new life elsewhere in North America.

*(Inset, top) Storefronts in Chinatown at the turn of the twentieth century. (Inset, bottom) Immigrants in traditional clothing were a common sight. (Above) Chinese grocers display their goods.*

his cousin's eyes were wide with fear. The driver would carry passengers to safety for fifty dollars a person. But Lung Tin claimed he only had enough money for one.

Hugh's eyes narrowed. He had watched Lung Tin gather up all the money from his father's store.

You're young, you're an American, you speak English, Lung Tin told Hugh. You don't have to be afraid of the future. Then he hopped onto the truck, and it drove away.

WATER. TO DORIS BEPLER, THAT WAS ALL THE GROWN-UPS WERE TALKING ABOUT. THERE WERE fires downtown, but the earthquake had broken the water pipes, and now there was no water to fight the flames.

Then her mother went to the sink to rinse the babies' diapers. She turned the faucet, but nothing came out.

Mr. Bepler wasted no time. He fetched two pails and handed them to Doris and Louise. They were to go to the well at the livery stable on Waller Street and bring back a few buckets so Mother could do the washing.

When they arrived at the stable, there was a line of people waiting with buckets, jugs, kettles, and dishpans.

"Do you think there'll be enough for us?" Doris asked her sister nervously.

"Don't worry, little girl," the stableman called out. "We'll keep pulling it up until the well runs dry."

*Water was no longer safe to drink or cook with unless it had been boiled.*

It was only two blocks back to the house, but it was a struggle with the heavy, full pails. The water kept sloshing over the sides. By the time they arrived home, Doris's high-laced shoes were soaked.

She dried off her shoes as best she could. Then she looked at the clock. It was almost time for her music lesson. She had arranged to have it early today. Aunt Anita was taking them to a picnic later, and Doris didn't want to miss it.

She gathered up her music and violin case and went downstairs. Her mother was sitting on the front steps with a few neighbors.

"Where are you going?" Mrs. Bepler asked.

"To my violin lesson. It's early today because of the picnic."

The women burst out laughing. There would be no music lesson today, her mother said, and no picnic either.

Doris didn't believe her. Her aunt had promised.

She headed down Noe Street to Aunt Anita's. On the way she saw Uncle Harry shaving right in his yard. He was trying to drain a garden faucet so he could fill his shaving mug. A trickle of brown water dribbled out of the tap.

She climbed the steep flight of stairs to Aunt Anita's third-floor flat. She begged her aunt to take them to the picnic as she had promised.

"Come out on the back porch," her aunt said. "And you'll see why we can't go."

The house was high on the hill and had a wide view of the whole of downtown San Francisco. But when Doris looked out toward the bay, all she could see was a mass of flames and black smoke rising into the clear blue sky.

"The city is on fire," her aunt said.

It was a strange sort of day. There was no proper lunch, and all day long they ate funny things, like leftover tapioca pudding with meringue on top. The grown-ups said they should fill up while they could. It was unlikely the bread man, the milkman, or the vegetable peddler would be making any deliveries for a while. Doris even watched one of her uncles break a raw egg into a cup and gulp it down whole.

She went to Duboce park with her sisters. As the hours passed, the sky changed. A cloud of gray smoke billowed up to the northeast. It reminded her of the genie in a story her father had once read to her.

Doris stopped running around when she saw the gray cloud. Instead she sat close to her sisters on the grass. They pulled a blanket over their heads to make a little shelter. Then they quietly sang every song and hymn they knew. Every once in a while Doris would poke her head out from under the blanket, hoping the dark cloud might have disappeared. But instead, each time, it seemed to draw closer.

*(Left) San Franciscans watch somberly as the downtown area is engulfed in smoke and flames. (Opposite) Doris witnesses the inferno from her aunt's back porch.*

More and more people came to the park. Some were all dressed up, the ladies even wearing their new Easter bonnets piled with bows and ostrich plumes. Others were fat with extra clothes, and several layers of skirts and petticoats stuck out beneath their coats.

Doris was happy to see the army trucks arrive. They drove straight into the park, making big ruts in the lawns and leaving muddy tracks on the tidy paths. Soldiers began putting up tents. In one of the big tents they stacked piles of blankets and folding cots. Doris and her sisters snuck in and began bouncing on the heaps and playing hide-and-seek around them, shrieking with laughter.

Then two men came in carrying a woman. It was a neighbor, Mrs. Wormser, and she was white and limp. She was a nurse and had been helping people in the park, but something bad had happened to her. As the men laid Mrs. Wormser gently on a cot, Doris made herself as small as possible and crawled back out under the flap of the tent. Then she hurried home. People were digging holes in their backyards, burying their china and silver and sewing machines.

Her father was in the dining room. Doris was about to go to him when she saw that he was sitting alone, very still. He was bent over, his face covered with his hands.

Doris suddenly felt very cold. She backed quietly out of the room. In the kitchen, she heard her mother talking softly to a neighbor.

Mr. Bepler's business partner had come to the house with terrible news. Her father's machine shop had burned to the ground. His business was completely gone.

Doris ran to her bedroom and closed the door. Then she sat in front of the dollhouse that she and her sisters had made out of orange crates. She began to tidy up the little house one room at a time. It made her feel good to set the tables and chairs upright again. But she was worried.

If the fire could burn down her father's shop, could it burn down their house, too?

❧

*A 1906 postcard shows San Franciscans camping out in a city park after the earthquake. Many of them had to remain there for several weeks or even months.*

## Earthquake and Fire

Earth's surface is divided into giant sections, or plates, which are constantly moving. The boundaries of these plates, called fault lines, run beneath land and ocean floors (figure 1). The San Andreas Fault, the longest in the world, stretches down the coast of California (figure 2).

In 1906, the two plates along the San Andreas Fault pushed against each other. The land on the western side of the fault shifted north (figure 3), causing an earthquake. Along the fault beaches sank, cliffsides crumbled, mines caved in, and entire redwood forests keeled over. One road moved almost twenty-one feet from its original position — the largest shift ever recorded.

In San Francisco, buildings crumbled. And all over town, fires broke out. Gas pipes ruptured, allowing gas to escape. Chimneys cracked and stoves were overturned, scattering hot coals and firewood. Kerosene lamps toppled to the ground and smashed. Electrical wires short-circuited. Vats of flammable chemicals were upended in drugstores and factories. Soon dozens of fires joined up, turning San Francisco into a raging firestorm.

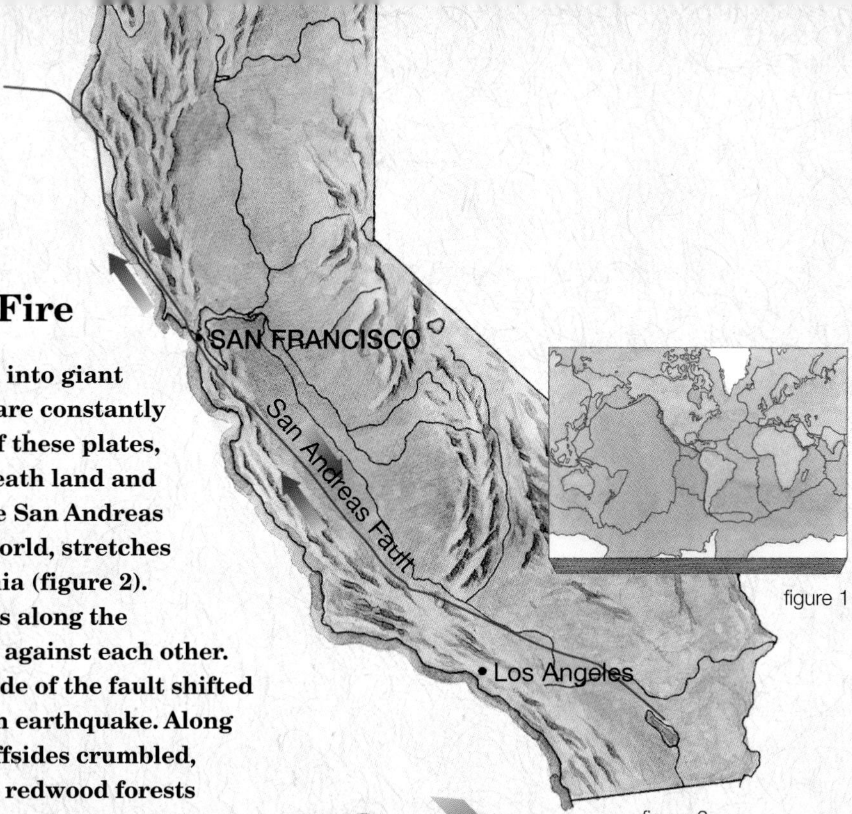

figure 1

figure 2

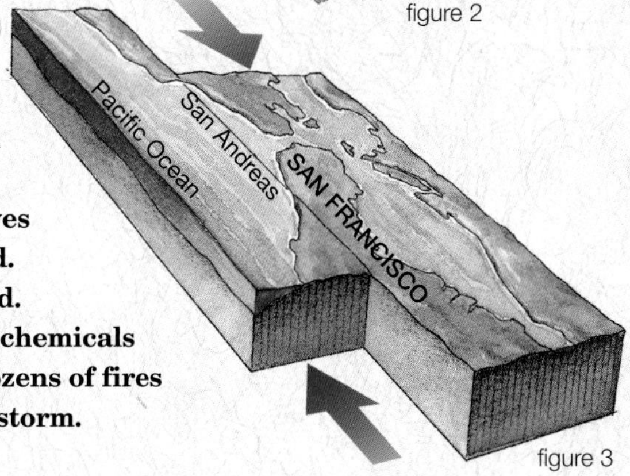

figure 3

## The Richter Scale

The Richter scale measures the amount of energy that an earthquake produces. The scale runs from zero to ten.

In the past two hundred years the biggest earthquake in the world occurred in Chile in 1960. It measured 9.5 on the Richter scale. The earth lurched so violently that giant waves called *tsunamis* raced across the Pacific Ocean, and fifty-foot waves crashed over the Hawaiian Islands 5,000 miles away.

But the biggest earthquakes are not always the deadliest. The heaviest casualties usually occur in densely populated areas where buildings are flimsy and rescue resources are poor. The deadliest earthquake in recent times occurred in China in 1976 and measured 8.0. The official death toll was 255,000, though it is believed the actual figure is close to 650,000. And in December 2003, an earthquake measuring 6.5 occurred in southwestern Iran, killing more than 25,000.

The 1906 San Francisco earthquake measured 8.3 on the Richter scale. More than 3,000 people died. The quake was thirty times more powerful than the 1989 San Francisco earthquake, which measured 7.1.

# CHAPTER THREE

# ESCAPE

Hugh Kwong Liang filled his father's old oak trunk with his belongings and pulled it out of the store.

The army had come and told everyone to leave Chinatown. The fires were getting too close. At first it seemed impossible that the fire could reach them, but now Market Street was a furnace of flame and smoke, and a fierce wind had come up.

There was little Hugh could do but follow the crowds of people out of Chinatown. It was hard to leave. His whole life was here. He walked past his old schools. The public school where he had learned English. The makeshift classroom where his father had sent him to study Chinese every afternoon, and each student had to bring a table and chair. The grammar school where he used to run for his life to get away from George Sterling, a tough kid who had once scratched Hugh's face with a penknife. Hugh still had the scar.

He dragged his father's trunk one block at a time up Nob Hill. The rope handle rubbed his hands raw. He saw a man nailing roller skates to the bottom of a trunk and wished he had done the same thing. The scraping sound of trunks being dragged over the pavement filled his head.

In the streets older Chinese women tottered on their small bound feet. Some wept quietly. On Sacramento Street a group of young girls poured out of the Presbyterian Mission Home. Almost everyone carried something — clothing and blankets or bags of rice — tied to broom handles with torn sheets and balanced across their shoulders. A few of the older girls carried babies on their backs. A tiny girl no older than five carefully held a basket of eggs in two hands.

❧

*(Opposite) From a vantage point on Nob Hill, Hugh takes a last look at Chinatown*
*before it is swallowed up by the fire.*

On Nob Hill, Hugh passed houses that looked like castles, with terraced gardens, wide windows, and turrets. One had marble lions guarding the entrance. Outside their gates, rich people packed up their belongings in a panic. Some had hired the horse-drawn wagons that the hog farmers used to collect wet garbage from the city's restaurants. Evil-smelling wet trails dripped from the back of wagons crammed with chandeliers, paintings, Persian rugs, and porcelain vases. A Chinese houseboy came out of a house carrying a mattress on his back. Another tended his two little charges, holding a baby in one arm and a toddler by the hand.

When Hugh reached the top of the hill, he stopped and looked back. He could see flames licking up over Chinatown, and he knew he would never see his home again.

Soldiers began to direct the refugees toward the open grounds of the Presidio Army Post on the outskirts of town. Some had bayonets fixed to their muskets, and the long blades gleamed sharply. At one point it seemed as though the entire army was thundering down Van Ness Avenue at a full gallop.

Hugh had never seen so many soldiers. Like most of the people of Chinatown, he was frightened of the authorities, and he stayed as far away from them as he could.

❦

*The beautiful mansions on Nob Hill (inset) were completely destroyed by fire. (Right) Some of the area's wealthy residents pull a wagon filled with their rescued belongings.*

*(Above) Tent cities sprang up all over San Francisco in the days following the quake, including this one at the Presidio Army Post. About 250,000 people, including this group at the Presidio (inset), were left homeless after the disaster.*

❧

They passed Lafayette Park, but it was already crowded, and there was no place to rest. There was no food or water either. Nothing to do but keep pressing on, away from the fire.

It was night by the time Hugh arrived at the Presidio. The army post had tents, blankets, and some water. Soldiers handed him a canvas tent and showed him how to put it up. A boy named Jimmy Ho stood nearby. He was sixteen and on his own, too, so Hugh asked him to share his tent. They put it up and placed Hugh's father's trunk inside. They had no other baggage.

Suddenly the boys heard a cry for help coming from a nearby tent. It was a young Chinese woman, and she was having a baby. Several older women gathered around to help her while her husband went in frantic search of a doctor.

The wind was so strong that sparks from the city fires were blowing over the camp. When Hugh and Jimmy realized the canvas of the woman's tent was getting very hot, they sprinkled water on it to stop it from catching fire.

But when they returned to their own tent, Hugh discovered that his father's trunk had been stolen. It was everything he had. He had dragged it clear across town.

It was the worst moment for both boys. Hungry, exhausted, and without a thing beyond the clothes on their backs, they broke into tears.

When Jimmy stopped sobbing, he told Hugh that he was going to go and look for his relatives. Many families had been separated. Perhaps they were somewhere in the camp. Then Jimmy said good-bye and went on his way, leaving Hugh in the tent, alone.

DeWitt Baldwin lost count of the fires as he made his way downtown, trying to get close to the action. The streets were clogged with tangled hoses, fallen wires, collapsed brickwork, and groups of onlookers. But he was a kid, and he slipped unnoticed through the crowds.

In the distance, the dome of San Francisco's City Hall stood against the sky. It had taken more than twenty years to build and cost seven million dollars. It was the city's pride and joy — the largest civic building outside Washington, D.C. Now you could see right through the dome, its frame as naked as a birdcage.

In some places DeWitt passed, it looked as though a giant had simply swatted at buildings with a huge hand. Whole walls had been sliced off, leaving bathtubs, tables, and toilets open to the street like the front of a dollhouse.

At Market and Valencia a man was pushing a piano along the road. When the man came to a halt at the streetcar tracks, he shrugged, told DeWitt he could have it, and continued on his way, leaving the piano abandoned in the middle of the street.

As the afternoon wore on, more and more people tried to leave

*The once-elegant City Hall (inset) was reduced to a hollow shell following the quake. It had to be demolished, and a new structure was built on the site. The redesigned city hall opened in 1915.*

*As thick smoke blankets the city skyline, only a few structures remain visible —
among them, the towering Ferry Building.*

⤙

the city. Crowds headed down Market Street to the Ferry Building. But when they got there, the ferries were full and would only carry passengers, not their baggage. So, many turned back, and soon the streets were clogged with people heading in all directions.

DeWitt started to notice the families. He saw boys his age carrying skates, bags of marbles, and slingshots. Worried mothers dragged small children by the hand and carried babies no older than his little sister.

DeWitt stopped walking. He had seen enough. He wanted to go home. So he turned around and joined the throng of people heading toward the hills beyond the Mission District.

NIGHT CAME, THOUGH IT WAS HARD TO TELL, BECAUSE THE SKY GREW BRIGHTER AND BRIGHTER AS the flames of the fire came closer.

Doris Bepler's father decided the family was no longer safe in the house. They would pack up what they could and walk west to Aunt Lou's house on Clayton Street.

They couldn't take much. The two babies were put in the carriage along with diapers, blankets, and the family silver. Then they all trudged up the Haight Street hill.

The hill was steep. Father had to carry six-year-old Beatrice from time to time. Mother made Doris and her sisters hold on to the side of the baby carriage or her skirt. The street

was filled with people fleeing the city, and she was afraid she would lose one of the girls in the crowd. Many were heading for Golden Gate Park, where the army was setting up tents and kitchens for the refugees.

All around them, families dragged pillowcases and blue-striped mattress covers stuffed with knobbly objects. One woman had an armful of pink and blue satin ball gowns. Two men carried a bathtub. Several people pushed sewing machines. One held a single frying pan, another a silver-topped walking stick. There were washtubs filled with silverware, wheelbarrows piled with dishes.

When they finally reached Aunt Lou's, they found that the chimney had fallen onto the roof and made a hole in the ceiling. So they sleepily dragged mattresses and blankets out onto the sidewalk. Neighbors had already pulled their stoves outside or made little cooking fires on the curb using bricks and old grates. Doris could smell coffee brewing. Someone was playing a banjo. It was almost as if they were at a picnic after all.

But she was so tired. She wrapped herself in a blanket and snuggled up against her sisters. Then she drifted to sleep as the glare from the flames turned the sky orange. Somewhere in the distance, she could hear the clanging of horse-drawn ambulances struggling to pull wagons of injured up the hills.

*After the quake, families cooked on makeshift stoves outside their homes (right). While many houses remained standing, their chimneys had collapsed, making cooking indoors impossible. (Below) This warped china teacup and saucer were recovered from a burnt-out home and kept as a souvenir.*

# CHAPTER FOUR

# HELP

**S**OL LESSER WOULD NOT BE GOING TO WORK. NOT TODAY, MAYBE NEVER. HIS HARDWARE store was in flames. Fires were burning all over downtown.

He wandered back to his neighborhood. Everywhere he turned, there was something terrible or hilarious to see. People standing at open windows, ready to jump from their flaming buildings. A cat being carried in a birdcage. A woman holding an ironing board and an iron. A family pushing all its belongings on a sofa with casters. Small monkeys scampering down the street, freed from a pet store at the corner of Bush and Kearny. A pile of bodies in a city park.

On Sacramento, people had pulled chairs onto the rubble-strewn street. They sat calmly on the slope of the hill gazing out at the black clouds like spectators at a fireworks display. From hour to hour, as the fire moved closer, they would simply move their chairs a bit farther up the hill. Some had driven in from the outskirts of town, and they strolled and pointed like tourists. Others posed for photographs, smiling as the smoke billowed up behind them. At every corner, kids ducked through the crowds, trying to get closer to the action.

But Sol wasn't a kid anymore. So he was happy when he heard that the city was organizing a relief committee. Anyone with a vehicle was to go to the Southern Pacific Railway Depot near the waterfront. Blankets, clothes, food, and tents would be arriving to be distributed to the needy.

At last he could do something to help. The only problem was, he didn't have a vehicle.

He finally found a dairy depot around the corner from his house. He persuaded the owner to lend him a horse-drawn milk wagon. Then he headed to the railway depot.

The journey was maddeningly slow. He had to guide his horse carefully around rough patches where cobblestones had popped out of the pavement. In many spots the streetcar

❧

*(Opposite) Sol carefully navigates his borrowed wagon along a broken cobblestone street.*

tracks had buckled. Sometimes they looked as though they had been sliced in two, with the broken ends sticking straight up. Desks and chairs had been pushed out of office buildings and abandoned in the middle of the street.

Two soldiers patrolled every block. The mayor had issued a proclamation saying that any looters would be shot on sight. The soldiers went into the saloons and poured all the liquor into the street. No one wanted anyone drinking at a time like this.

As the night wore on, firefighters began to collapse from heat and exhaustion. Some dozed, slumped in a doorway or against their equipment, before getting up to continue the battle. Some beat at the flames with blankets and clothing. Useless fire hoses lay in tangled heaps.

On the south side of Market Street, the Palace Hotel was no more. It had been the most famous hotel in the city, where you could see rich men in silk hats and ladies wearing diamonds on every finger. Its architects had boasted that the hotel could withstand both earthquake and fire. It had been built on massive foundations twelve feet deep, with walls that were two feet thick and reinforced by iron strips. The basement had held an enormous water tank, and 130,000 gallons more had been stored in six tanks on the roof.

Inside, no luxury had been spared. There were Turkish carpets, glittering chandeliers, marble sinks, redwood-paneled elevators, and a magnificent palm-filled courtyard with a glass roof. Just the night before, Enrico Caruso, the

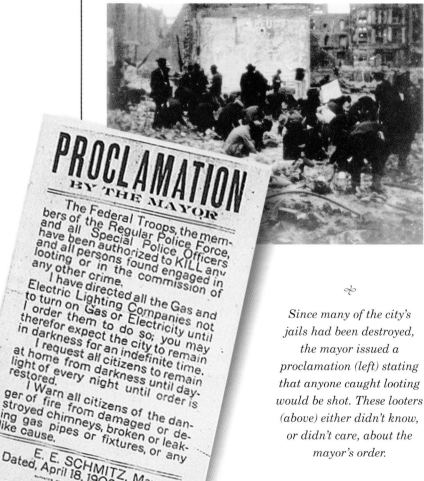

*❧*

*Since many of the city's jails had been destroyed, the mayor issued a proclamation (left) stating that anyone caught looting would be shot. These looters (above) either didn't know, or didn't care, about the mayor's order.*

34

*World-famous tenor Enrico Caruso (left) was thrown from his bed in the Palace Hotel (above) but managed to flee to safety. (Right) As firefighters watch helplessly, flames shoot from the windows of the Call Building.*

greatest singer in the world, had slept in his luxurious room on the fifth floor after a magnificent performance of *Carmen* at the Grand Opera House next door. Now the hotel was a ruin, the water supply long gone. Caruso had left the city, never to return.

Sometimes the heat was so intense that Sol could not make his horse move forward, and he had to zigzag his way to the railway depot. The streets were clogged with rubble, and even the newfangled automobiles were moving at a snail's pace.

At Mission and First a heap of dead cattle lay in the middle of the street. Two blocks away, the Call Building was alight. The windows on the fourth floor had blown out, and the whole building had turned into a furnace, sucking air up to its dome, which burst into flames. Below, firefighters had watched helplessly as the fire slowly worked its way down to the ground, one floor at a time.

At Mission and Fifth, armed soldiers circled the U.S. Mint. People brought their belongings and piled them around the building, feeling sure their things would be safe there. *(Continued on page 38.)*

# San Francisco's Fire Horses

In 1906, firefighters used horses to haul their pumps, ladders, and hoses. The horses had to be high-spirited and eager to work, but not easily spooked by clanging bells or panicky humans. They had to be strong enough to pull 10,000 pounds of heavy equipment up San Francisco's steep hills, but nimble enough to manage the slippery cobblestone streets (the horses wore shoes with rubber heels to help them keep their footing). They had to be able to back up properly and, on command, to step quickly into a harness suspended from above. (One crew boasted they could have a horse harnessed and ready to go in seven and a half seconds.)

In exchange for their hard work and obedience, fire horses were treated like kings. Their stalls were always airy, comfortable, and perfectly clean. After each fire, their nostrils and eyes were gently sponged. Some were served hot porridge every morning.

Many fire horses were devoted to their keepers. One was so fond of his driver that he followed him up the stairs of the fire hall, and the crew could not make him go back down. Eventually they had to remove a second-story window and rig a pulley to lower the horse to the ground.

The keepers were devoted to the horses, too. When one driver steered his horse into a shop window to keep his wagon from hitting a cable car full of passengers, the horse's jugular vein was cut. Though a policeman wanted to shoot the dying horse, the driver held the two ends of the vein together until a doctor came to stitch up the blood vessel. The horse eventually went back to work wearing an impressive scar.

Fire horses served bravely in the 1906 fire. Some worked until they collapsed from heat or fatigue, their harnesses almost seared to their sides.

In 1912, horses began to be replaced by vehicles, and in 1921, the last San Francisco fire horse was retired.

(*Continued from page 35.*) And they were. Inside, the Mint employees had remained at their posts, even when the windows turned bright red and exploded, and burning embers rained down overhead. They formed a chain and carried buckets of water from the well in the courtyard, wetting down the hot roof and exposed rafters. Seven hours later, the fires were out, and $200 million had been saved.

Finally Sol reached the depot. Miraculously, it had been saved from fire because water had been pumped out of the channel that cut behind it from the bay.

He was given a white bandage with a red cross on it. Someone had scrawled the words "Relief Committee" on the bandage.

Sol loaded up his wagon with bread, cookies, canned goods, and milk. Then he began to make his way back across town. He was to deliver his supplies to Lafayette Park. It was in his neighborhood, just four blocks from his house.

When he turned in to the park, the hills were dotted with men, women, and children

(*Above*) *Supplies are given out at a relief station set up in one of San Francisco's parks. Within days of the disaster, donations began arriving from all over the country. Relief Committee workers wore armbands with red crosses hastily sewn on (right).*

camping under tents made out of bedsheets, blankets, and carpets. People swarmed over the sides of the wagon, grabbing anything they could carry. Within minutes the wagon was empty.

There was nothing to do but turn the horse around and make another trip back to the depot.

It was clear that no one would sleep much tonight.

NIGHT HAD FALLEN, BUT THE SKY WAS SO BRIGHT THAT YOU COULD READ A BOOK BY THE LIGHT from the flames. In the distance, Hugh Liang could see that the fire was sweeping to the northwest, straight toward the Presidio. If it kept coming, soon the entire peninsula would be in flames.

He did not want to burn to death.

He began to walk through the sea of tents. Chinese, whites, young, and old milled around. Many were sleeping, exhausted by their trek across town. Others just sat on their bundles and stared at the ground. He could smell bread baking and coffee brewing. Soldiers watched every move.

Hugh kept walking toward the water. At least then he could leap into the bay if the fire caught up with him. Even drowning would be better than burning to death.

He spotted a light flashing in the distance. When he drew closer he saw soldiers at a wharf carrying supplies from a boat to two army trucks. During a moment when they were busy at the trucks, he quickly sneaked onto the boat, stumbled below, and hid under a table.

Not much later, Hugh felt the boat begin to move. He trembled with fear. White soldiers with guns. What would they do to him if they found him? The noise of heavy footsteps drew closer. The light was turned on. He was in the galley, and the men were looking for something to eat.

"Look!" one soldier yelled suddenly. He dragged Hugh out from under the table. Soon the boy was surrounded by a half dozen men, and the captain was questioning him sternly.

He told them the whole story. Lung Tin, and Jimmy. The fire in Chinatown, and his flight across town. The stolen trunk that had belonged to his father. His voice shook. He was terrified of what these men would do to him. But the men just told him that everything would be all right, and that he shouldn't worry. They offered him food. It was the first time he had eaten in more than twenty-four hours. They gave him meat, vegetables, and coffee. Then they told him to clean up the galley.

He was more than happy to do it.

# The 1906 Earthquake and Fire

The earthquake affected nearly every part of San Francisco, but the fire was concentrated mainly in the downtown area (shown in gray on the map below). The inferno created gale-force winds as it sucked up oxygen, and reached a peak temperature of 2,700 degrees Fahrenheit. It was only on the morning of the fourth day that firefighters finally managed to put out the last of the blaze. By then, nearly a quarter of the city was a charred ruin.

It is estimated that three thousand people died in the disaster. Property damage was valued at around $400 million — more than $8 billion in today's money.

**1.** Golden Gate Park. A field hospital was set up here, which eventually treated over five thousand patients. Today the park contains the city's only public memorial to the quake — the front porch of a grand home that once stood on Nob Hill.

**2.** The Presidio Army Post. Immediately after the disaster, the situation was desperate for many refugees, who had little or no water, food, or shelter. The Presidio's four supply depots managed to distribute three thousand tents during the first three days, as well as temporary shelters and clothing.

**3.** Duboce Park. From here, Doris Bepler and her sisters watched the smoke from the downtown fires turn the sky black.

Sacramento Street

Sutter Street

Noe Street

**4.** **Valencia Street Hotel.** DeWitt Baldwin witnessed a horrific scene here. The four-story structure, built on a swamp, essentially sank, trapping a lot of people. Many of these victims drowned in the stagnant swamp or in water from a burst water main. Only a dozen people were rescued.

**5.** **Southern Pacific Railway Depot.** In addition to serving as a supply warehouse where Sol Lesser and other volunteers picked up goods to distribute to refugees, the depot was also a gateway out of the devastated city. Between April 18 and April 22, almost half the population (225,000 people) fled San Francisco by train and boat — the largest evacuation of an American city during peacetime.

**6.** **City Hall.** San Francisco's pride and joy had opened just seven years earlier. Although the structure was badly damaged, some of its offices reopened and were used until 1909, when the building was demolished.

**7.** **Call Building.** The building survived intact despite extensive fire damage, and still stands proudly on Market Street today.

**8.** **Ferry Building.** Beginning in the first few hours after the quake, and continuing through the days that followed, boats leaving from the Ferry Building carried refugees across San Francisco Bay to safety. In all, about 20,000 people were rescued by boat.

**9.** **Chinatown.** This small area was home to 60,000 Chinese immigrants, who were not always welcome in their new homeland. In the month after the quake, most Chinese refugees had been sent to camps outside of the city. The mayor formed a committee to find a new location for Chinatown — ideally, far outside downtown. Only pressure from the Empress-Dowager of China put an end to the relocation scheme. Present-day Chinatown remains in its original spot.

**10.** **Nob Hill.** Many of San Francisco's wealthy citizens lived in luxurious homes here. Hugh Liang saw residents trying to save their expensive belongings before abandoning the neighborhood. Unfortunately, most of the mansions on the hill burned to the ground in the fire that ravaged downtown.

**11.** **Lafayette Park.** By the time Hugh passed this park, it was so crowded with refugees that he could not stop there. In fact, the city's parks housed more than 200,000 refugees for months and, in some cases, years. The last refugee camp did not close until 1909.

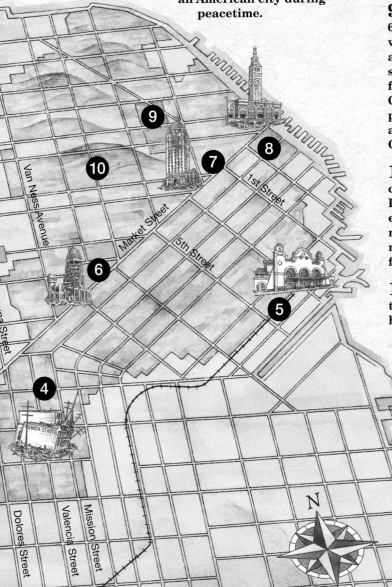

# FROM THE ASHES

THE SAN FRANCISCO FIRE RAGED FOR THREE DAYS AND NIGHTS, EATING ITS WAY THROUGH almost five hundred city blocks. It destroyed some of the waterfront, all of the business district, all of Chinatown, and all the grand mansions on Nob Hill. It swallowed a fresh block of buildings every fifteen minutes and threw up billowing clouds of smoke that could be seen nearly one hundred miles out to sea.

The city looked and sounded like a war zone. Buildings were deliberately blown up to create a wide trench that the flames could not cross. Some of these explosions accidentally caused new fires, as burning debris flew out of buildings like flaming missiles. But in the end, the firebreak worked. The last flames were put out early Saturday morning, April 21 — seventy-four hours after the fire started. That night, heavy rains began to fall.

When the smoke cleared, one-quarter of the city was a blackened skeleton of twisted metal, stumps of chimneys and walls, charred timbers, and endless heaps of rubble. For weeks the air was filled with a fine powder of dust and ashes. All the familiar billboards and shop signs were gone.

The fire was stopped just a few blocks from the houses of DeWitt Baldwin, Doris Bepler, and Sol Lesser. But 250,000 people were not so lucky. More than four square miles

of the city had been destroyed. Within this area, only a few tiny pockets were saved, including the U.S. Mint and the Post Office, where ten employees beat out flames with dampened mail sacks. Not a single piece of mail in the building was lost.

The fire wiped out Chinatown, including Hugh Liang's home. Hugh was taken across the bay by boat. Before he went ashore, the men on board took up a collection and gave him the money, along with their good wishes. He never forgot their kindness.

All along the bay, large and small communities opened their homes to the thousands who were forced to leave the city with only the clothes on their backs. Many of the refugees had lost their businesses as well. After days of poking through the ruins of his burnt-out machine shop, Doris Bepler's father finally found the company safe. It was still so hot inside that when he opened the door and air rushed in, the papers burst into flames, and a pile of gold and silver coins melted into a solid mass.

For weeks after the flames had died, water was more precious than gold. In some places it sold for fifty cents a glass. In the parks and camps, huge cauldrons of water were boiled, and people lined up for hours to fill their jugs and buckets. People dug pits in their backyards and hung sheets around them instead of using their toilets. Broken sewer lines had polluted the city's water supply, and officials were afraid that disease would spread. Water was to be used for cooking and drinking only. Not a drop could be wasted.

News of the disaster traveled across the country and around the world. Americans everywhere immediately did whatever they could to help. Students in Oregon baked hundreds of loaves of bread. Texans sent meat. The newly organized Red Cross was sent in and became recognized as the leader of large-scale relief in America. Doctors, nurses, medical supplies, food, and money poured in from every state. Big signs on the sides of incoming railway cars brought cheery messages — "Keep your chins up, Frisco! We're with you!" It would not be the last time Americans would wholeheartedly reach out to help their countrymen.

Ten days after the earthquake, most people had food and shelter, and thoughts quickly turned to rebuilding the city. The new San Francisco would be more beautiful and stronger than ever, with wide streets and modern buildings made of steel frames and concrete.

Chinatown was one of the first neighborhoods to begin rebuilding. The community worked night and day to clear away debris and erect new structures, using unburned bricks that were carefully collected from the ruins. The narrow, dark streets and alleys were widened and paved. There were new schools, a hospital, and shiny storefronts with big glass windows. Tourists came to the bright restaurants, grocery stores, and shops. Families resettled. Today, San Francisco's Chinatown remains the heart of the Chinese community in the United States.

*(Above) Nob Hill, where the city's finest mansions once stood, was now an empty wasteland. (Page 42–43) Crumbled buildings and heaps of rubble are all that remain at the intersection of Turk and Market Streets.*

The rebuilding of the rest of the city quickly followed. Everyone pitched in. Some schools did not open for several months, so many children spent their time collecting useful junk from the ruins — copper wire, lead pipes, and dishes. Some cleaned bricks for a dollar an hour.

More than ten million cubic yards of rubble had to be removed before any reconstruction could begin. Much of the rubble was shoveled into Mission Bay to create more land. Many of San Francisco's new buildings now stand on this filled land, and some experts wonder whether these buildings can survive another great earthquake.

The city's firefighting powers were also improved. Huge water reservoirs were dug into the hills. Pumping stations were built on solid bedrock to pull salt water from the bay. Extra hydrants were installed. Today more than 150 underground cisterns made of reinforced concrete are clearly marked by rings of bricks embedded in the pavement.

Meanwhile, the city continues to be shaken by earthquakes, though nothing has come close to matching the power of the 1906 quake. But no one seems too worried. Today San Francisco has a population of more than one million people, and is considered one of the most beautiful and exciting cities in the world.

LIKE THE BOMBING OF PEARL HARBOR, THE assassination of John F. Kennedy, and the terrorist attacks of September 11, the San Francisco earthquake was an event that made all Americans sit up and pay attention. The photos of the mighty city in flames; the scenes of skyscrapers, homes, and businesses turned into burnt rubble overnight; and the news that 250,000 fellow Americans were now homeless shocked the whole nation. And, in the end, the disaster made everyone ask difficult questions.

What would it be like to lose everything? What is our most precious possession? Who is in charge when catastrophe strikes? How safe are we? Whose fault is it? How can we stop disaster next time?

And what can be done when the disaster is caused by the earth itself, constantly alive and moving, right beneath our feet?

## True Stories

Hugh Kwong Liang, Doris Bepler, Sol Lesser, and DeWitt Baldwin all survived the San Francisco earthquake, and many years later they told their stories. As young children, Doris and DeWitt were spared some of the terror that the grown-ups around them no doubt felt. They remember their parents being calm and trying to make life as normal as possible. "As an eight-year-old boy, I was not frightened then by the actual earthquake," DeWitt said eighty-two years later. "My attitude was one of excitement, curiosity, and a great desire to see and hear all I could."

Even for older children, the day sometimes seemed unreal. Sol Lesser said, "I wasn't troubled by the disaster at the moment. It was more like some story or book." One of his most vivid memories was being allowed by police to raid a candy store before it was dynamited. He and a dozen neighborhood kids helped themselves to boxes of jelly beans, jujubes, chocolate, and all-day suckers and loaded them all into a cable-car caboose that they pushed three blocks up the hill.

But the trauma of a stressful situation and the passage of time can color people's memories. The tiniest details might remain sharp (many years later, Doris Bepler remembered her broken shoelace, and the exact songs she and her sisters sang in the park), while entire days can blur together. Sol Lesser, for example, remembered delivering supplies from the railway depot on the night of April 18, though historians say supplies did not in fact arrive until the following day.

One thing is certain. April 18, 1906, was a day that would never be forgotten by those who survived it, young and old alike.

# GLOSSARY

**boardinghouse**: a house where meals and living quarters are provided for a fee.

**cable car**: a passenger vehicle that runs on rails and is pulled along by a moving cable laid into the road.

**casualties**: people who are killed or injured in an accident, disaster, or during a battle.

**cistern**: an underground tank for storing rainwater.

**cobblestone**: a rounded paving stone.

**flannelette**: cotton fabric made to imitate the feel of flannel.

**kerosene**: an oil burned in lamps and other heating and lighting devices.

**mah-jongg**: a Chinese four-person game played with tiles.

**peninsula**: a strip of land that juts out into water.

**petticoat**: a skirt or dress worn as an undergarment.

**reservoir**: a natural or artificial lake holding a supply of water.

**streetcar**: a passenger vehicle that runs on rails, similar to a **cable car**; however, a streetcar contains its own motor and draws power from an overhead electrical cable.

**water main**: a main pipeline of a city's water distribution system.

# INDEX

## PICTURE CREDITS

## FIRST-HAND ACCOUNTS

**DeWitt Baldwin**: San Francisco History Center, San Francisco Public Library, "Memories of the San Francisco Earthquake and Fire" by DeWitt C. Baldwin as related to Ana Maria P. de Jesus, September 19, 1988.

**Sol Lesser**: California Historical Society, Manuscript Collection, MS 699. "My Experiences During the Earthquake and Fire in San Francisco, April 18, 1906" by Sol Lesser.

**Hugh Kwong Liang**: San Diego Chinese Historical Society and Museum newsletters: Fall 1995, Winter 1996, and Spring 1996. "Excerpts from the Life Story of Hugh Kwong Liang" by Murray K. Lee.

**Doris Sharp** [nee Bepler]: California Historical Society, Manuscript Collection MS 3501. "I Was There, April 18, 1906" by Doris Sharp, 1976.

## RECOMMENDED READING

*For young readers:*

**Earthquake in the Early Morning (Magic Tree House series)** by Mary Pope Osbourne (Random House). Series heroes Jack and Annie travel through time to San Francisco on the morning of April 18, 1906, just before the earthquake.

**Quake! Disaster in San Francisco, 1906** by Gail Langer Karwoski (Peachtree). A boy struggles to find his family amid the chaos.

*For older readers:*

**Denial of Disaster: The Untold Story and Photographs of the San Francisco Earthquake of 1906** by Gladys Hansen and Emmet Condon (Cameron and Company). A detailed and highly illustrated history of the disaster and its immediate and long-term consequences.

**Disaster! The Great San Francisco Earthquake and Fire of 1906** by Dan Kurzman (Perennial). A deeply researched account of this historic calamity.

**The Firehorses of San Francisco** by Natlee Kenoyer (Westernlore Press). The unique history of San Franciso's gallant firehorses.

## WEBSITES

**The California Historical Society** www.californiahistoricalsociety.org

**U.S. Geological Survey: 1906 San Francisco Quake** quake.wr.usgs.gov/info/1906

**The Virtual Museum of the City of San Francisco** www.sfmuseum.org

## ACKNOWLEDGMENTS

The author and Madison Press Books would like to thank Mireille Majoor for her tireless research on our behalf. We would also like to acknowledge the assistance of Murray K. Lee at the San Diego Chinese Historical Society and Museum; Joe Evans and the staff of the North Baker Research Library at the California Historical Society; and Judy De Bella and Richard Hansen at the Virtual Museum of the City of San Francisco (sfmuseum.org).

*Chairman and Founder:*
Albert E.Cummings

*President and CEO:*
Brian Soye

*Editorial Director:*
Hugh M. Brewster

*Associate Editorial Director:*
Wanda Nowakowska

*Project Editor:*
Imoinda Romain

*Editorial Assistance:*
Catherine Fraccaro
Shima Aoki

*Graphic Designer:*
Jennifer Lum

*Production Director:*
Susan Barrable

*Production Manager:*
Donna Chong

*Printing and Binding:*
Tien Wah Press

Madison Press Books
1000 Yonge Street, Suite 200, Toronto, Ontario
Canada, M4W 2K2